George and the Dragon

By

Michael Fitzalan

GEORGE and the DRAGON

By

Michael Fitzalan

You come readily on the hour.

Synopsis

Bobby, a painter is repainting a pub when he finds a cache of sovereigns and some bonds. He visits a broker that he knows through family connections. She listens to his story, but there is a twist. A gang of villains using a courier company as a front has discovered the haul too. Gina insists that Bobby return the cash to the crooks. Before he has an opportunity, they are on to him. He is pursued by the gang and one falls off scaffolding chasing him another into the river, third off a tube platform and fourth gets run over. Bobby enjoys the craic after the first one. Three to go. Then the tail kidnaps Georgina. Bobby gives himself up in hope that they will let her go if the money is returned. He winds up in a disused furniture veneer factory with a chain saw running towards him. George is tied up in the office. The motor of the chain saw starts up and the saw moves up between his legs. Helpless George waits to hear the scream. Can anyone of anything save them?

Scene 1

2 painters in overalls sitting on two firkins. Sitting out in sunshine near to a set of open cellar flaps. They're eating their lunch.

Bobby:

"It sticks in my throat like the fur ball in the throat of a tom cat, or the corn in the gullet of a Foie Gras goose."

Paul:

"What's that mate?"

Bobby:

"The people from the agency sending a chap like you on a job like this."

Paul:

"What do you mean?"

Bobby:

"Will you look at the neat, convenient size of you? How tall are you?"

Paul:

"Five foot three and a half."

Bobby:

"Precisely. And how tall are the ceilings in that pub?"

Paul:

“I’d say about nine foot”.

Bobby:

“Indeed. So how did they think you were going to reach the ceiling with your paint brush?”

Paul:

“It’s all right. The cellar is only about seven foot high. I can reach that just, and I can always stand on a barrel if I feel like it”.

Bobby:

“Ah, it’s grand being poor. It makes you inventive and self-reliant, full of initiative. Still, it’s not easy being rich. I reckon they have less money for the table than us, with all the healthcare and family saving plans and the insurance. Being poor, you die early so there’s no worry.”

Paul:

“Is that so? My Gran’s ninety.”

Bobby:

“If you live hard and you’re poor you die early. It was in the paper only the other day”.

Paul:

“They warned me about you at the agency. You’re a hard-drinking man and you’ll do your liver in before you’re fifty.”

Bobby:

"Well, I have ten good years left then, and I won't have to worry about me pension. If only I'd been smarter. I invented a roller to do the ceilings, which allowed the brush to sink back into a little tray that caught the paint, and mop up any of the spills. I could have made a fortune with that particular contraption, but I kept it to myself for too long and didn't someone come along and patent the idea. I'll never make my fortune now. I'm too old. I'm too tired. I've lost the fight."

Paul:

"You're not doing too badly for yourself old man."

Bobby:

"Less of the old. And I'll have you know, I'm a happy man if I have a roof over my head, food in my bell, a stout pair of boots. That and the money for five pints of stout at the end of the day. I wouldn't want to be you starting off now, in this world."

Paul:

"I'm all right. I've got me family. I've got this job. My Dad always said if you have a trade, you'll never be hungry. Talking of which, I've got peanut butter, brown sauce, and marmalade in my sandwich. What have you got in yours?"

Bobby:

"I won't swap one of my rounds for your diabolical concoction. Cheese and pickle for me. A plough man's lunch and the hands of a plough man. I wish at times that my soul was as white as the emulsion we're putting on the cellar ceiling."

Paul:

"So what did you do before you painted?"

Bobby:

"I did lots of jobs. One of them was an extra for an English actor in a west coast film. There's not a man from Galway to Kinsale who hasn't at one time stood in the shoes of a great actor. Your man wasn't a great actor; he was an old soft porn star. Then he worked in the musicals. I still see his car when I pass his flat in Clapham. I wonder whether he's bought the flat yet or whether he's still renting. I'm sure he had loads of money, but he never owned a house in England. It must have been a tax dodge. It's a funny thing when you think about it. He drives a big brown Chevrolet when he should be driving one hell of a Dodge."

Paul:

"My Auntie Edie, she was an extra in an episode of East Enders."

Bobby:

"Well that's as maybe, but we're not going to get the same rates as the filum stars, and we won't get paid for this job if we hang about chatting all day. You finish that sandwich and I'll go and prep the party wall so we can put a good coat on before we do the ceiling, and I'll be waiting for the first to dry on the ceiling."

Paul:

"Don't you want the rest of your sandwich?"

Bobby:

"You have that half. You're a growing lad. I've grown in several different directions. I think my growing days are over. I get all the nourishment I need from the old-fashioned kind of stout."

Paul:

"Cheers. I'll buy you a pint when we've finished the job on Friday."

Bobby:

"How old are you?"

Paul:

"N-n-n-n-n-nineteen."

Bobby:

"Well you're old enough to drink half a gallon a night, and you can buy the first pint tonight. The overtime that I pay you on this job will allow you to stand the old man a good few pints."

Bobby disappears down into the cellar, Paul munches happily on the cheese sandwich.

Bobby calls up:

"Paul, can you come down here as soon as you can. I need you to help with moving some bricks."

There is silence while Paul scoffs his silence.

Paul:

"I'll be down in a mo."

Cut to Bobby down in the cellar picking bricks away with his hands to reveal money sacks with £20 printed on the side.

He claws away at the sacks to get them open. Puts up a screen. Sends Bobby to get some cigarettes so he can't discover the haul.

Scene 2

Outside on the street in Bermondsey. Bobby into mobile phone.

Bobby:

"Georgina! How the hell are your?"

Gina:

"Yes, I'm fine Bobby. What's new?"

Bobby:

"I was just passing and I wanted to have a little chat with your. Are you free for a few minutes?

Gina

You can come up briefly if you like, but I'm going out tonight. I was just about to get changed. I won't be long, and I'll run the bath for you while we're talking.

Bobby retraces his steps from Number 19 to Number 11 and leans heavily on the button that reads Flat A. He gives a satisfied smile as he hears the soft padding of her footsteps on the other side of her door. The door opens to reveal a gorgeous blonde girl with brown eyes, small stud earrings, a red top, a faux expensive watch and black pencil skirt with what could be stockings or tights, and a pair of trendy uncomfortable shoes.

Gina:

“That was quick.”

Bobby:

“And you didn’t keep me waiting either. It sounded like a ballerina coming down those stairs. I hardly heard your.”

Gina:

“Don’t pretend that you’ve forgotten that I once was. And even ballerinas with all the attention they get know that they need more flattery than that before they let an Irishman like you darken their doorstep.”

Bobby:

“Well, you can talk out here if you like. That’s if you don’t trust me. But I’ve always preferred to gas away with a pot of brown tea and a slice of bread and butter. If that’s not asking too much of a fine lady like yourself.”

Gina:

“You can dispense with the old blarney. It might work with naïve colleens where you come from, if they’re 15 and don’t know any better. But it doesn’t work in a grand metropolis like London.”

Bobby:

“I miss our sparkly conversation, and you’d be surprised how much an ounce of Irish charm can buy your on these streets that some *idjet* (idiot) told me were paved with gold.Are you going to let me in? Or am I going to the park to walk and talk to the ducks?”

Gina:

"I'll let you in this time because I'm curious. It's not often that you come round here without calling first three days in advance for a supper date that will involve you being ten minutes early, and plying me with booze."

They walk up the stairs to the flat. Bobby leans on the mantle piece which is covered with invitations.

Bobby:

"Have you lost weight since I last saw your?"

Gina:

"Take a chair Bobby. Would you like a drink?"

Bobby sits on the sofa while Georgina moves to a wooden table on which is a tray containing spirits, minerals and a stainless steel ice bucket.

Bobby:

"I'd love one. Will your join me?"

Gina:

"Just a brandy and soda to settle my stomach."

Bobby:

"That's my girl. My old grandfather never went out in the evening without a glass of milk to line his stomach. And he never made any journey beyond the threshold without a brandy and soda to bring down the blood pressure."

Gina:

"I remember Bobby. You always tell the same old story ten thousand times. You're lucky that there are girls like me who never tire of the stories from the old country."

Bobby:

"Ha well. If I'm boring you, I'd best be on my way. But I'll have the brandy and soda first. There's nothing like a brandy to keep your spirits up and you blood pressure low.

Georgina fixes the drinks on a table in front of the sofa where Bobby sits with his hands on his knees and his legs wide open as if he's about to pounce.

Gina:

"Cheers."

Bobby:

"*Slante*. So is your eating enough? You do look kind of thin, but I know you've always liked to be that way. They do say back in the old country that the nearer the bone, the sweeter the meat."

Gina:

"And I've seen you walk down the road, see a pretty girl, and say nice from far and far from nice. I've heard them all. I've been through your repertoire almost as often as you have."

Bobby:

"You can be cruel when you want to be. I'm just seriously concerned that you're keeping well."

Gina:

"I'm eating very healthily thank you. I eat loads of fruit, and rice."

Bobby:

"Do you still have a good appetite?"

There is a pause

Gina:

"You're disgusting. All you think about is drink, food and your own carnal needs. You're an omathon."

Bobby

That's unkind, but I suppose it's fair. At my age you know, you've only got another ten or so good years of it, so you pull out the stops.

Gina

We'll remain platonic, Bobby, but don't stop trying, it's good practice.

Bobby

I'll drink my drink and be a good boy and I'll tell you a story.

Gina

Go ahead, I like a good yarn.

Bobby

Now, usually, I don't let the truth get in the way of a good story, but this one is gospel. There was a man in the thirties, seventh son of a seventh son. He married a beautiful girl from Clair and he was an R.I.C. man.

Gina

R.I.C?

Bobby

They were the police force. The Royal Irish constabulary. They kept the peace as far as possible. Separating the locals from the army. Irishmen in the pay of a foreign government. A tricky task during the troubles and the Civil War after. His marriage saved him form a bullet. Only a relationship with a local girl could save a government official from the Republican snipers. Any way, when everything was over, he had a choice a pension or a lump sum. He took the money and the boat to Liverpool. He worked in a bar in Clapham.

Gina

Which one?

Bobby

Does it matter? The Falcon. Then he bought his first pub and by the outbreak of war, he had five pubs. The war came and he put his money into whiskey in bonded warehouses. After the war he sold it at a huge profit. One of his city pubs got bombed and he got more cash. By the time he retired he had fifteen pubs in London and fifteen in Dublin. One of them, the biggest Guinness retail outlet in the world. He spent seven year in Portugal to avoid paying tax.

Gina

What happened?

Bobby

After a gatherer comes a scatterer. One of his sons spent all the money. They sold the last place to another Irish fella who had two pubs already.

Gina

That's a great story but where do you come in?

Bobby

I'm painting the Head Office. Top to bottom, there's a pub underneath and a portion of the cellar goes under the road. While I was down there the wall collapsed.

Gina

Don't tell me you found gold.

Bobby

Not quite, I found something better. Bags of silver coins.

Gina

Old sovereigns?

Bobby

That's right, but there's more. I found a cache of bonds in a steel case. The old man had stashed away some extra cash for his descendants but they never were bothered to find it.

There worth a fortune.

Gina
How do you know the bonds are worth anything?

Bobby

I love the Reference Library. You know that's where I learn everything.

Gina

So you want me to launder you money?

Bobby

Who better than a high flier in the city who knows all the right people and can put the cash offshore?

Gina

That's stealing.

Bobby

It's ill gotten gains, purloined from the tax man.

Gina

It's still theft.

Bobby

Not in my book. Do you know Ashford castle?

Gina

I've been to a conference there, two hundred plus a night and views over the Corrib and the Mask beyond.

Bobby

There lovely Lochs we used to take the train to Galway when I was a lad. We'd head from there for a spot of fishing. I had an aunt in Balinrobe.

Gina

I know we've had this conversation before.

Bobby

Sorry. What I didn't tell you was the Guinness family owned the place, built it at a cost of one million pounds. They had a flying boat that they took from Dublin harbour and they landed in the Corrib.

Gina

You're rambling again.

Bobby

Not at all, they sold the place. Rumour has it that they were fed up of their silver being pinched.

Gina

Purloined.

Bobby

Precisely

Gina aghast

So you want me to be your banker?

Bobby, *appeasing with hands and voice.*

I'll give you a percentage. Your bonus wasn't as big as last year, so the papers say. Your lifestyle hasn't changed; you're still out every night.

Gina

Mostly on business, as I am tonight.

Bobby

I won't keep you much longer. I'm afraid there *is* a catch.

Gina

I thought so.

Bobby

It's a big one. I found out that I'm not the only one who knows about the bonds.

Gina

You better get in quick. My meter's running.

Bobby

These fellas I don't want to compete with. I looked up the lease on the place next door, number three. It belongs to Dragon Trading.

Gina

Sounds like a Chinese operation, you're not involved with the Triads?

Bobby

Worse the Dragon is a gang. The Jefe, he's a mean character he breathes fire. Then you have the four legs, henchmen who do a light bit of stomping on people. Then, you have the really ruthless one, he's the tail. He makes sure people get the point. People don't expect a dragon to use its tail, but they're dead before they know it.

Gina

Bobby, what have you done?

Bobby

We'll I took the chest, didn't I? I could only have one hit.

Gina

Did you take the bags as well?

Bobby

Some.

Gina

Come on, how many?

Bobby

About fourteen, it's my lucky number.

Gina

Not now, it's not.

Bobby

I've finished the job.

Gina

So that's okay, is that what you're going to tell me?

Bobby

No, it's not.

Gina

Spill, Bobby.

Bobby

They're smart people, you don't survive in their game without a little bit up here.

Gina

Tell me something I don't know.

Bobby

We'll it's only a matter of time. You see they'll lean on the manager and then they'll learn I had access to the cellar.

Gina

Your good at covering your tracks aren't you? At least where the income tax man is concerned.

Bobby

You're right, but the job was too big for me and I used some agency boys. A different one every day and a different agency, but one of them will talk.

Gina

We don't have much time. We have to get you liquid and out of here.

Bobby

I have enough liquidity in my glass and I've always liked to be near where you are.

Gina

I've listened to your tale and I've waited while my bath water has gone cold. Our historical links are through family connections, so let's keep it that way. I've been telling you to put aside some of your beer money for years. There's no get rich quick method. I've worked seven days a week for three years to get what I have and I'm not going to risk it all by getting involved in your crooked deals. These guys sound worse than the Mafia. Give them back their soiled money and walk away.

Bobby

I can always rely on you for what the Americans call a reality check. You're right of course. I just had a dream of hanging up the brush.

Gina

Dream on. You come within a mile of me without returning all their ill gotten gains and you'll wish they'd caught up with you. There's your hat, what's you hurry.

Bobby

You're not the first to give me the bum's rush. I know when I'm not welcome.

Gina

Don't give me that lost boy crap. I know you too well. Go and sort out your life. I don't need the extra aggravation.

Bobby

I'm sorry my visit caused you so much vexation.

Gina

You're not vexing me, wild colonial boy. You know the right thing to do. So do it. Weren't you the one who taught me that honesty was the best policy?

Bobby

I was a better man then.

Gina

I know you'll never get over Peggy's death, but you're still the same fine man underneath those bent bonds.

Bobby

A man needs a wife to keep him on track

Gina

Don't get corny on me Bob. Any woman only needs to take care of herself, and men have to try to be that strong. If they were you wouldn't be asking me questions that you know the answers to already.

Bobby

You're right as usual.

Gina

Don't give me any old flannel. Save your patronising for someone with less sense. Someone really dense.

Bobby

You're a tough lady.

Gina

There's no other type worth knowing.

Bobby

You're a good girl.

Gina

And your better than you know, don't be a fool, sort it out.

Bobby

Exit stage left, Take care Georgina

Gina

You take care, too, Robert Fitzgerald, of Offlay, my Errant Knight. You've helped me out many times before and now I'm helping you. Drop it. Do yourself a favour.

Scene 3

Cut to smoke filled room in basement West end couriers' office back room in the shadow of the Telecom tower.

First henchman has gone to get a brandy and soda from the pub next door and has returned with a tray. The Dragon is chain smoking Player's non-filter. Smoke billows from his mouth.

Dragon

You know I hate profanity of any kind. All the kids saying see you next Tuesday on the corners and all vat. But some git has been raiding my stash and I'm not sure I like it. F.B. He's only gone and taken the chest that was my reserve fund.

Henchman one

Don't spill your drink guv. That'll be the third glass you've swiped off the table.

Dragon

You blooming frigging minx, I paid for the drinks I'll do what I like. If I wanted a wife I would have stuck with Diana, Cor, she was the Princess of Wails, I can tell yah. Stop being a wus. Sit it and shut it. I pay good money for you to listen to me you flaming wally. What are you doing about getting my money back? I yanked your tutu out of the Repton Club, set you up and you give me naafink.

Henchman 2

We've talked to the governor of the pub, boss, and he reckons it was some painters he had in.

Dragon

I'll give you painters. You're about as much use as women when they've got the painters in. You a sodding waste of space. Two days since we've made our discovery and you come up with that. You're worse than useless. You're sodding useless. Come on Sherlock, A Blood Hound could have told me more by wagging its wotsit.

Henchmen three (Liverpudlian)

Calm done boss, we done better than the busys, I swear to god. We know the face and we got everyone scouring the town.

Dragon

You Scousers could do with some scouring. Kin Hell why did I ever think it was worth having a friend from the north?

Henchman 3

You're all right with me, boss, this fella's a Mick. They call Liverpool Little Dublin and he works in the building game. I've got friends, contacts; they'll track him down before you can say Liverpool beat Arsenal.

Dragon

That's why I pay you. Connections, contacts, the station's up the road mate. I want you to get off your Arsenal and get some results.

Henchman 2

We will boss.

Dragon

I ate yesterday, I'm hungry today. Get this guy, bring him to me, and get him now!

Henchmen 1

We will boss. Take it easy. Remember what the doctor said about your heart.

Dragon tossing a one pound coin on the table.

Sod my f-in' heart. What do you see on the coin?

Henchman One, leaning over the coin.

I see the queen.

Dragon

Well done, now flip it over.

Henchman one *reluctantly and slowly turns the coin over.*

It's a dragon

Dragon

That's right, give the boy a gold star. See that tongue hanging out? That's me. I've got a frigging fork tongue. You are my legs; you do all the donkey work. That dragon has strong legs and they've got claws on them. You four are like pigeons, weak legs, stubby claws, and full of it. See that tail. You know about him don't you. There's a sharp point there and you'll be feeling it soon. We were flying until this character tried to clip our wings. I want results today. Otherwise you'll be visited from the tail and believe me you'll get his point even if you've missed mine.

Henchman three

But boss we're on to him….

Dragon

Spare me, he's not dealt with. Deal with him now, or we'll have to cut you like a deck of cards. You with me? Earn your money. Sling it. I want results and I get what I want.

Now get out, pee off with you, and don't darken my door until you have that Spud and whoever helped him. Got it? I want this boy to suffer, ordeal by fire and by smoke. He'll be dragging himself around with scaly skin for the rest of his life. Mark my words. Now shift

Scene 3.

Henchman 2 is sitting in the bar of a down at heal pub in Tooting watching a game of pool on a raised dais. On the table opposite sits Bobby, quietly supping his beer.

H2 moving to the table.

Hello Bobby.

Bobby

Do I know you?

H2

It was a while back, the job you did in Chiswell Street.

Bobby

The job I did with Pat Murphy.

H2

That's the one

Bobby

It was a long hot job that one, the sun blistered your skin. I don't recall any Scousers on the job. You must have been sub-contracted by Steve O'Connell.

H2

That's right can I get you a Guinness

Bobby

No thank you, I only have two pints night, that's all that's good for you. Everything in moderation. I have a reputation but I never live up to it.

H2

I know what you mean, you can have too much of a good thing. You must have got that reputation somehow.

Bobby

Indeed, I know most of the publicans in the Greater London area, but I never cause trouble. Because you're known people think you must live there. Especially, a single man with no wife to go home to, but I always leave the party at its height.

H2

One more want do you any harm, just this once.

Bobby

I have few rules in my life but there are two I stick by. One, I never have more than two pints, I have to bit fit for work and the second is I always get the first round in.

H2

That sounds good to me.

Bobby

No doubt it does but I'm not in the habit of buying drinks for strangers.

H2

Well, I never came to the pub on that job because I was on antibiotics.

Bobby

I never heard of a Liverpudlian giving up booze because they take some pills. That Chiswell Street job was during the worse thunder storms that I can remember. The plasterers were sent home for three days because the roof sprang a leak and the gutters hadn't been fixed properly. Steve O'Connell is a postman. There's no O'Connell in the building game. So, I'll ask you again, do I know you?

H2

You don't, but I heard you had come into to some money.

Bobby

Where did you hear that nonsense?

H2

From the dragon who wants it back.

Bobby

So you're one of the legs, I wondered when you would walk into my life. I should hop it if I were you.

H2

You should be on the stage, you're so funny. I was never keen on Mick humour.

Bobby

Maybe that's because you don't understand it.

H2

I understand it; I just don't find it funny.

Bobby

Each to their own.

H2

Let's get down to business, there are three more of us, and we'll all pay you a visit if you don't co-operate. I'm asking you nicely to give the money back. You leave town and we promise that we won't come after you.

Bobby

Do you mind if I smoke?

H2

Of course you can, have one of mine

Offers a Marlboro Light.

Bobby

Thank you, but you can keep your coffin nails. I smoke cigars. You can't beat the taste of an awld cheroot. I packed in fags years ago. As Mark Twain said, 'A woman is a woman but a cigar is a good smoke.'

H2

Smoke whatever you want and we'll discuss how you can give us back our money.

Bobby

You can give me a light this old petrol lighter is no good, it's always packing in.

H2

There you go. Now, as I was saying, there's a hard way and easy way but we'll get our money back.

Bobby

I need to fill my lighter as we talk; I always carry around a tin of lighter fuel to keep the old Zippo stoked up. You carry on.

H2

The money.

Bobby

Indeed, now, strictly speaking it's not yours, it belongs to the awld fella who had the pub. It's not yours and I dare say it's not moine, but possession is nine tenths of the law and I seem to have possession.

H2

Don't come the crafty old Irish git with me.

Bobby spills the contents of the petrol lighter.

H2

Hey, what did you do that for you stupid bugger?

Bobby striking the Zippo and watching the flame.

Now, lighter fuel is an interesting substance. You can pour it on your arm and light it straight away and it will evaporate as it burns. However it gets messy when you involve cotton and the detergent in the fabric. You're soaked in the stuff. It's being absorbed into the skin. I just have to drop the lighter and you'll go up like a roman candle.

H2

You're a mad old git.

Bobby

This mad old git always leaves the party at its height. I'll be off and you won't follow me if you know what's good for you. A pity as I liked the old pub. Enjoy your lager and I'll be on my way.

Bobby stands and runs to the door. H2 sits looking at his drenched clothes and then runs after Bobby. There is a pause as the Juke box volume rises to a crescendo, I want to Break Free by Freddie Mercury. A minute passes. Bobby re-enters the pub.

Bobby to barmaid.

I think I'll have one for the road.

Barmaid

But you never have more than two pints.

Bobby

I think I'll make this an exception, I've just seen a man run over. Call an ambulance when you get a chance.

www.ingramcontent.com/pod-product-compliance
Ingram Content Group UK Ltd.
Pitfield, Milton Keynes, MK11 3LW, UK
UKHW041903190726
13854UKWH00003B/1069

9 781447 799207